They

"I DON'T KNOW WHAT I SHOULD HAVE DONE WITHOUT TALLIES."—p. 68.

BY

RUDYARD KIPLING

.

WITH ILLUSTRATIONS BY F. H. TOWNSEND

London
MACMILLAN AND CO., Limited
1905

ILLUSTRATIONS

THE RETURN OF THE CHILDREN

Neither the harps nor the crowns amused, nor the
    cherubs' dove-winged races—
Holding hands forlornly the Children wandered beneath
    the Dome ;
Plucking the radiant robes of the passers-by, and with
    pitiful faces
Begging what Princes and Powers refused :—'Ah,
    please will you let us go home ?'

Over the jewelled floor, nigh weeping, ran to them
    Mary the Mother,
Kneeled and caressed and made promise with kisses,
    and drew them along to the gateway—
Yea, the all-iron unbribeable Door which Peter must
    guard and none other—
Straightway She took the Keys from his keeping, and
    opened and freed them straightway.

Then to Her Son, Who had seen and smiled, She said :
    'On the night that I bore Thee,
What didst Thou care for a love beyond mine or a
    heaven that was not my arm ?
Didst Thou push from the nipple, O Child, to hear
    the angels adore Thee ?
When we two lay in the breath of the kine ?' And
    He said :—'Thou hast done no harm.'

So through the Void the Children ran homeward
    merrily hand in hand,
Looking neither to left nor right where the breathless
    Heavens stood still ;
And the Guards of the Void resheathed their swords,
    for they heard the Command :
'Shall I that have suffered the children to come to me
    hold them against their will ?'

'THEY'

ONE view called me to another; one
hill top to its fellow, half across the
county, and since I could answer at no
more trouble than the snapping forward
of a lever, I let the county flow under
my wheels. The orchid-studded flats
of the East gave way to the thyme, ilex,
and grey grass of the Downs; these
again to the rich cornland and fig-trees
of the lower coast, where you carry the
beat of the tide on your left hand for
fifteen level miles; and when, at last,
I turned inland through a huddle of
rounded hills and woods I had run
myself clean out of my known marks.

𝔈   7

Beyond that precise hamlet which stands
godmother to the capital of the United
States, I found hidden villages where
bees, the only things awake, boomed in
eighty-foot lindens that overhung grey
Norman churches ; miraculous brooks
diving under stone bridges built for
heavier traffic than would ever vex them
again ; tithe-barns larger than their
churches, and an old smithy that cried
out aloud how it had once been a hall
of the Knights of the Temple.   Gipsies
I met on a common where the gorse,
brackens, and heath fought it out together up a mile of Roman road ; and
a little farther on I disturbed a red fox
rolling dog-fashion in the naked sunlight.

As the wooded hills closed about me
I stood up in the car to take the bear-
ings of that great Down whose ringed
head is a landmark for fifty miles across

the low countries. I judged that the
lie of the country would bring me across
some westward-running road that went
to his feet, but I did not allow for the
confusing veils of the woods. A quick
turn plunged me first into a green cut-
ting brim-full of liquid sunshine; next
into a gloomy tunnel where last year's
dead leaves whispered and scuffled
about my tyres. The strong hazel stuff
meeting overhead had not been cut for
a couple of generations at least, nor had
any axe helped the moss-cankered oak
and beech to spring above them. Here
the road changed frankly into a carpeted
ride on whose brown velvet spent
primrose-clumps showed like jade, and
a few sickly, white-stalked blue-bells
nodded together. As the slope favoured
I shut off the power and slid over the
whirled leaves, expecting every moment
to meet a keeper ; but I only heard a

jay, far off, arguing against the silence
under the twilight of the trees.

Still the track descended. I was on the
point of reversing and working my way
back as best I could ere I ended in some
swamp, when I saw sunshine through
the tangle ahead and lifted the brake.

It was down again at once. As the
light beat across my face my fore-wheels
took the turf of a smooth still lawn from
which sprang horsemen ten feet high
with levelled lances, monstrous peacocks,
and sleek round-headed maids of honour
—blue, black, and glistening—all of
clipped yew. Across the lawn—the
marshalled woods besieged it on three
sides—stood an ancient house of lichened
and weather-worn stone, with mullioned
windows and roofs of rose-red tile. It
was flanked by semi-circular walls, also
rose-red, that closed the lawn to the
fourth side, and at their feet a box hedge

B

grew man-high.   There were doves on
the roof about the slim brick chimneys,
and I caught a glimpse of an octagonal
dove-house behind the screening wall.

Here, then, I stayed ; a horseman's
green spear laid at my breast ; held by
the exceeding beauty of that jewel in
that setting.

'If I am not packed off for a trespasser,
or if this knight does not ride a wallop
at me,' thought I, 'Shakespeare and
Queen Elizabeth will come out of that
half-open garden door and ask me to
tea.'

A child appeared at an upper window,
and I thought the little thing waved a
friendly hand.   But it was to call a
companion, for presently another bright
head showed.   Then I heard a laugh
among the yew-peacocks, and turning
to make sure (till then I had been
watching the house only) saw the

silver of a fountain behind a hedge
thrown up against the sun.   The doves
on the roof cooed to the cooing water ;
but between the two notes I caught
the utterly happy chuckle of a child
absorbed in some light mischief.

The garden door—heavy oak sunk
deep in the thickness of the wall—
opened further : a woman in a big
garden hat set her foot slowly on the
time-hollowed stone steps and slowly
walked across the turf.   I was forming
some apology when she lifted her head
and I saw that she was blind.

' I heard you,' she said.   ' Isn't that
a motor car ? '

' I'm afraid I've made a mistake in
my road.   I should have turned off up
above—I never dreamed——' I began.

' But I'm very glad.   Fancy a motor
car coming into the garden !   It will
be such a treat——' She turned and

SHE TURNED AND MADE AS THOUGH LOOKING ABOUT HER.

made as though looking about her. 'You — you haven't seen any one, have you—perhaps ?'

'No one to speak to, but the children seemed interested at a distance.'

'Which ?'

'I saw a couple up at the window just now, and I think I heard a little chap in the grounds.'

'Oh, lucky you !' she cried, and her face brightened. 'I hear them, of course, but that's all. You've seen them and heard them ?'

'Yes,' I answered. 'And if I know anything of children, one of them's having a beautiful time by the fountain yonder. Escaped, I imagine.'

'You're fond of children ?'

I gave her one or two reasons why I did not altogether hate them.

'Of course, of course,' she said. 'Then you understand. Then you

won't think it foolish if I ask you to
take your car through the gardens, once
or twice—quite slowly? I'm sure they'd
like to see it. They see so little, poor
things. One tries to make their life
pleasant, but——' she threw out her
hands towards the woods. 'We're so
out of the world here.'

'That will be splendid,' I said. 'But
I mustn't cut up your grass.'

She faced to the right. 'Wait a
minute,' said she. 'We're at the South
gate, aren't we? Behind those peacocks
there's a flagged path. We call it the
Peacocks' Walk. You can't see it from
here, they tell me, but if you squeeze
along by the edge of the wood you can
turn at the first peacock and get on to
the flags.'

It was sacrilege to wake that dream-
ing house-front with the clatter of
machinery, but I swung the car to clear

the turf, brushed along the edge of the
wood and turned in on the broad stone
path where the fountain-basin lay like
one star-sapphire.

'May I come too ?' she cried. 'No,
please don't help me. They'll like it
better if they see me.'

She felt her way lightly to the front
of the car, and with one foot on the step
she called : 'Children, oh, children !
Look and see what's going to happen !'

The voice would have drawn lost
souls from the Pit, for the yearning that
underlay its sweetness, and I was not
surprised to hear an answering shout
behind the yews. It must have been
the child by the fountain, but he fled at
our approach, leaving a little toy boat
in the water. I saw the glint of his
blue blouse among the still horsemen.

Very disposedly we paraded the
length of the walk and at her request

HE FLED AT OUR APPROACH.

backed again. This time the child had got the better of his panic, but stood far off and doubting.

'The little fellow's watching us,' I said. 'I wonder if he'd like a ride.'

'They're very shy still. Very shy. But, oh, lucky you to be able to see them ! Let's listen.'

I stopped the machine at once, and. the humid stillness, heavy with the scent of box, cloaked us deep. Shears I could hear where some gardener was clipping, a mumble of bees, and broken voices that might have been the doves.

'Oh, unkind !' she said weariedly.

'Perhaps they're only shy of the motor. That little maid at the window looks tremendously interested.'

'Yes ?' She raised her head. 'It was wrong of me to say that. They are really fond of me. It's the only thing that makes life worth living—

when they're fond of you, isn't it?
I daren't think what the place would
be without them. By the way, is it
beautiful?'

'I think it is the most beautiful place
I have ever seen.'

'So they all tell me. I can feel it,
of course, but that isn't quite the same
thing.'

'Then have you never —— ?' I
began, but stopped abashed.

'Not since I can remember. It
happened when I was only a few months
old, they tell me. And yet I must
remember something, else how could I
dream about colours. I see light in my
dreams, and colours, but I never see
them. I only hear them, just as I do
when I'm awake.'

'It's difficult to see faces in dreams.
Some people can, but most of us haven't
the gift,' I went on, looking up at the

window where the child stood all but hidden.

'I've heard that too,' she said. 'And they tell me that one never sees a dead person's face in a dream. Is that true?'

'I believe it is—now I come to think of it.'

'But how is it with yourself—yourself?' The blind eyes turned towards me.

'I have never seen the faces of my dead in any dream,' I answered.

'Then it must be as bad as being blind.'

The sun had dipped behind the woods and the long shades were possessing the insolent horsemen one by one. I saw the light die from off the top of a glossy-leaved lance and all its brave hard green turn to soft black. The house, accepting another day at end, as it had accepted an hundred thousand

c

gone, seemed to settle deeper into its rest among the shadows.

'Have you ever wanted to ?' she said after the silence.

'Very much sometimes,' I replied. The child had left the window as the shadows shut upon it.

'Ah!   So've I, but I don't suppose it's allowed. . . . Where d'you live ?'

'Quite the other side of the county —sixty miles and more, and I must be going back.   I've come without my big lamps.'

'But it's not dark yet.   I can feel it.'

'I'm afraid it will be by the time I get home.   Could you lend me some one to set me on my road at first ?   I've utterly lost myself.'

'I'll send Madden with you to the cross-roads.   We are so out of the

world, I don't wonder you were lost. I'll guide you round to the front of the house ; but you *will* go slowly, won't you, till you're out of the grounds ? It isn't foolish, do you think ? '

' I promise you I'll go like this,' I said, and let the car start herself down the flagged path.

We skirted the left wing of the house, whose elaborately cast lead guttering alone was worth a day's journey ; passed under a great rose-grown gate in the red wall, and so round to the high front of the house which in beauty and stateliness as much excelled the back as that all others I had seen.

' Is it so very beautiful ? ' she said wistfully when she heard my raptures. ' And you like the lead-figures too ? There's the old azalea garden behind. They say that this place must have been made for children. Will you help me

out, please? I should like to come
with you as far as the cross-roads, but
I mustn't leave them. Is that you,
Madden? I want you to show this
gentleman the way to the cross-roads.
He has lost his way but—he has seen
them.'

A butler appeared noiselessly at the
miracle of old oak that must be called
the front door, and slipped aside to put
on his hat. She stood looking at me
with open blue eyes in which no sight
lay; and I saw for the first time that
she was beautiful.

'Remember,' she said quietly, 'if
you are fond of them you will come
again,' and disappeared within the
house.

The butler in the car said nothing
till we were nearly at the lodge gates,
where catching a glimpse of a blue
blouse in a shrubbery I swerved amply

I SWERVED AMPLY LEST THE DEVIL THAT LEADS LITTLE BOYS TO PLAY SHOULD
DRAG ME INTO CHILD-MURDER.

lest the devil that leads little boys to
play should drag me into child-murder.

'Excuse me,' he asked of a sudden,
'but why did you do that, Sir?'

'The child yonder.'

'Our young gentleman in blue?'

'Of course.'

'He runs about a good deal. Did
you see him by the fountain, Sir?'

'Oh, yes, several times. Do we turn
here?'

'Yes, Sir. And did you 'appen to
see them upstairs too?'

'At the upper window? Yes.'

'Was that before the mistress come
out to speak to you, Sir?'

'A little before that. Why d'you
want to know?'

He paused a little. 'Only to make
sure that—that they had seen the car,
Sir, because with children running
about, though I'm sure you're driving

particularly careful, there might be an accident. That was all, Sir. Here are the cross-roads. You can't miss your way from now on. Thank you, Sir, but that isn't *our* custom, not with———'

'I beg your pardon,' I said, and thrust away the British silver.

'Oh, it's quite right with the rest of 'em as a rule. Good-bye, Sir.'

He retired into the armour-plated conning-tower of his caste and walked away. Evidently a butler solicitous for the honour of the house, and interested, probably through a maid, in its nursery.

Once beyond the signposts at the cross-roads I looked back, but the crumpled hills interlaced so jealously that I could not see where the house had lain. When I asked its name at a cottage along the road, the fat woman who sold sweetmeats there gave me to

understand that people with motor cars
had small right to live—much less to
'go about talking like carriage folk.'
They were not a pleasant - mannered
community.

As I retraced my run on the
map that evening I was little wiser.
Hawkin's Old Farm appeared to be
the Survey title of the place, and the
old County Gazetteer, generally so
ample, did not allude to it. The big
house of those parts was Hodnington
Hall, Georgian with early Victorian
embellishments, as an atrocious steel
engraving attested. I carried my diffi-
culty to a neighbour—a deep-rooted
tree of that soil—and he gave me a
name of a family which conveyed no
meaning.

A month or so later I went again—
or it may have been that my car took
the road of her own volition. She

over-ran the fruitless Downs, threaded
every turn of the maze of lanes below
the hills, drew through the high-walled
woods, impenetrable in their full leaf,
came out at the cross-roads where the
butler had left me, and a little farther
on developed an internal trouble which
forced me to turn her in on a grass
way-waste that cut into a summer-silent
hazel wood. So far as I could make
sure by the sun and a six-inch Ordnance
map, this should be the road-flank of
that wood which I had first explored
from the heights above. I made a
mighty serious business of my repairs
and a glittering shop of my repair-kit,
spanners, pump, and the like, which I
spread out orderly upon a rug. It was
a trap to catch all childhood, for on
such a day, I argued, the children would
not be far off. When I paused in my
work I listened, but the wood was so

IT WAS A TRAP TO CATCH ALL CHILDHOOD, FOR ON SUCH A DAY, I ARGUED,
THE CHILDREN WOULD NOT BE FAR OFF.

full of the noises of summer (though
the birds had mated) that I could
not at first distinguish these from the
tread of small cautious feet stealing
across the dead leaves. I rang my bell
in an alluring manner, but the feet fled,
and I repented, for to a child a sudden
noise is very real terror. I must have
been at work half an hour when I heard
in the wood the voice of the blind
woman crying : 'Children, oh, children !
Where are you ?' and the stillness made
slow to close on the perfection of that
cry. She came towards me, half feeling
her way between the tree-boles, and
though a child, it seemed, clung to her
skirt, it swerved into the leafage like a
rabbit as she drew nearer.

'Is that you ?' she said. 'From the
other side of the county ?'

'Yes, it's me—from the other side of
the county.'

'Then why didn't you come through the upper woods? They were there just now.'

'They were here a few minutes ago. I expect they knew my car had broken down, and came to see the fun.'

'Nothing serious, I hope? How do cars break down?'

'In fifty different ways. Only mine has chosen the fifty first.'

She laughed merrily at the tiny joke, cooed with delicious laughter, and pushed her hat back.

'Let me hear,' she said.

'Wait a moment,' I cried, 'and I'll get you a cushion.'

She set her foot on the rug all covered with spare parts, and stooped above it eagerly. 'What delightful things!' The hands through which she saw glanced in the chequered sunlight. 'A box here—another box!

Why you've arranged them like playing shop !'

'I confess now that I put it out to
attract them. I don't need half those
things really.'

'How nice of you ! I heard your
bell in the upper wood. You say they
were here before that ?'

'I'm sure of it. Why are they so
shy ? That little fellow in blue who
was with you just now ought to have
got over his fright. He's been watching
me like a Red Indian.'

'It must have been your bell,' she
said. 'I heard one of them go past me
in trouble when I was coming down.
They're shy — so shy even with me.'
She turned her face over her shoulder
and cried again : 'Children, oh, children ! Look and see !'

'They must have gone off together
on their own affairs,' I suggested, for

"WHY YOU'VE ARRANGED THEM LIKE PLAYING SHOP!"

there was a murmur behind us of
lowered voices broken by the sudden
squawking giggles of childhood. I returned to my tinkerings and she leaned
forward, her chin on her hand, listening
interestedly.

' How many are they ? ' I said at last.
My work was finished, but I saw no
reason to go.

Her forehead puckered a little in
thought. ' I don't quite know,' she
said simply. ' Sometimes more—sometimes less. They come and stay with
me because I love them, you see.'

' That must be very jolly,' I said,
replacing a drawer, and as I spoke I
heard the inanity of my answer.

' You—you aren't laughing at me,'
she cried. ' I—I haven't any of my
own. I never married. People laugh
at me sometimes about them because—
because—'

'Because they're savages,' I returned. 'It's nothing to fret for. That sort laugh at everything that isn't in their own fat lives.'

I don't know. How should I ? I only don't like being laughed at about *them*. It hurts ; and when one can't see. . . . I don't want to seem silly,' her chin quivered like a child's as she spoke, 'but we blindies have only one skin, I think. Everything outside hits straight at our souls. It's different with you. You've such good defences in your eyes—looking out—before any one can really pain you in your soul. People forget that with us.'

I was silent reviewing that inexhaustible matter—the more than inherited (since it is also carefully taught) brutality of the Christian peoples, beside which the mere heathendom of the West Coast nigger is clean and restrained.

It led me a long distance into myself.

'Don't do that !' she said of a sudden,
putting her hands before her eyes.

'What ?'

She made a gesture with her hand.

'That !   It's—it's all purple and
black. Don't !   That colour hurts.'

'But, how in the world do you know
about colours ?' I exclaimed, for here
was a revelation indeed.

'Colours as colours ?' she asked.

'No. *Those* Colours which you saw
just now.'

'You know as well as I do,' she
laughed, 'else you wouldn't have asked
that question.   They aren't in the
world at all.   They're in *you*—when
you went so angry.'

'D'you mean dull purplish patches,
like port wine mixed with ink ?' I said.

'I've never seen ink or port wine,

but the colours aren't mixed.   They
are separate—all separate.'

'Do you mean black streaks and jags
across the purple ?'

She nodded.   'Yes—if they are like
this,' and zig-zagged her finger again,
'but it's more red than purple—that
bad colour.'

'And what are the colours at the top
of the—whatever you see ?'

Slowly she leaned forward and traced
on the rug the figure of the Egg itself.

'I see them so,' she said, pointing
with a grass stem, 'white, green, yellow,
red, purple, and when people are angry
or bad, black across the red—as you
were just now.'

'Who told you anything about it—
in the beginning ?' I demanded.

'About the Colours ?   No one.   I
used to ask what colours were when I
was little—in table-covers and curtains

and carpets, you see — because some
colours hurt me and some made me
happy. People told me ; and when I
got older that was how I saw people.'
Again she traced the outline of the Egg
which it is given to very few of us to
see.

'All by yourself ? ' I repeated.

'All by myself. There wasn't any
one else. I only found out afterwards
that other people did not see the
Colours.'

She leaned against the tree-bole
plaiting and unplaiting chance-plucked
grass stems. The children in the wood
had drawn nearer. I could see them,
with the tail of my eye, frolicking like
squirrels.

'Now I am sure you will never
laugh at me,' she went on after a long
silence. 'Nor at *them*.'

'Goodness—no ! ' I cried, jolted

out of my train of thought. 'A man
who laughs at a child—unless the child
is laughing too—is a heathen !'

'I didn't mean that, of course.
You'd never laugh *at* children, but I
thought—I used to think—that perhaps
you might laugh about *them*. So now
I beg your pardon. . . . What are you
going to laugh at ?'

I had made no sound, but she
knew.

'At the notion of your begging my
pardon. If you had done your duty as
a pillar of the State and a landed pro-
prietress you ought to have summoned
me for trespass when I barged through
your woods the other day. It was dis-
graceful of me—inexcusable.'

She looked at me, her head against
the tree trunk—long and steadfastly—
this woman who could see the naked
soul.

'How curious,' she half whispered. 'How very curious.'

'Why, what have I done?'

'You don't understand . . . and yet you understood about the Colours. Don't you understand?'

She spoke with a passion that nothing had justified, and I faced her bewilderedly as she rose. The children had gathered themselves in a roundel behind a bramble bush. One sleek head bent over something smaller, and the set of the little shoulders told me that fingers were on lips. They, too, had some child's tremendous secret. I alone was hopelessly astray there in the broad sunlight.

'No,' I said, and shook my head as though the dead eyes could note. 'Whatever it is, I don't understand yet. Perhaps I shall later—if you'll let me come again.'

' You will come again,' she answered.
' You will surely come again and walk
in the wood.'

' Perhaps the children will know me
well enough by that time to let me play
with them—as a favour. You know
what children are like.'

' It isn't a matter of favour but of
right,' she replied, and while I wondered
what she meant, a dishevelled woman
plunged round the bend of the road,
loose-haired, purple, almost lowing with
agony as she ran. It was my rude, fat
friend of the sweetmeat shop. The
blind woman heard and stepped forward.
' What is it, Mrs. Madehurst ? ' she
asked.

The woman flung her apron over her
head and literally grovelled in the dust,
crying that her grandchild was sick to
death, that the local doctor was away
fishing, that Jenny the mother was at

THE WOMAN FLUNG HER APRON OVER HER HEAD AND LITERALLY GROVELLED IN
THE DUST.

her wits' end, and so forth, with repeti-
tions and bellowings.

'Where's the next nearest doctor?'
I asked between paroxysms.

'Madden will tell you. Go round
to the house and take him with you.
I'll attend to this. Be quick!' She
half supported the fat woman into the
shade. In two minutes I was blowing
all the horns of Jericho under the front
of the House Beautiful, and Madden,
from the pantry, rose to the crisis like a
butler and a man.

A quarter of an hour at illegal
speeds caught us a doctor five miles
away. Within the half-hour we had
decanted him, much interested in
motors, at the door of the sweetmeat
shop, and drew up the road to await
the verdict.

'Useful things cars,' said Madden,
all man and no butler. 'If I'd had one

when mine took sick she wouldn't have died.'

'How was it ?' I asked.

'Croup. Mrs. Madden was away. No one knew what to do. I drove eight miles in a tax-cart for the doctor. She was choked when we came back. This car 'd ha' saved her. She'd have been close on ten now.'

'I'm sorry,' I said. 'I thought you were rather fond of children from what you told me going to the cross-roads the other day.'

'Have you seen 'em again, Sir—this mornin' ? '

'Yes, but they're well broke to cars. I couldn't get any of them within twenty yards of it.'

He looked at me carefully as a scout considers a stranger—not as a menial should lift his eyes to his divinely appointed superior.

'I wonder why,' he said just above the breath that he drew.

We waited on. A light wind from the sea faltered up and down the long lines of the woods, and the way-side grasses, whitened already with summer dust, rose and bowed in sallow waves.

A woman, wiping the suds off her arms, came out of the cottage next the sweetmeat shop.

'I've be'n listenin' in de back-yard,' she said cheerily. 'He says Arthur's unaccountable bad. Did ye hear him shruck just now? Unaccountable bad. I reckon t'will come Jenny's turn to walk in de wood nex' week along, Mr. Madden.'

'Excuse me, Sir, but your lap-robe is slipping,' said Madden deferentially. The woman started, dropped a curtsey, and hurried away.

'What does she mean by "walking in the wood"?' I asked.

'It must be some saying they use hereabouts. I'm from Norfolk myself,' said Madden. 'They're an independent lot in this county. She took you for a chauffeur, Sir.'

I saw the Doctor come out of the cottage followed by a draggle-tailed wench who clung to his arm as though he could make treaty for her with Death. 'Dat sort,' she wailed—'dey're just as much to us dat has 'em as if dey was lawful born. Just as much—just as much! An' God he'd be just as pleased if you saved 'un, Doctor. Don't take it from me. Miss Florence will tell ye de very same. Don't leave 'im, Doctor!'

'I know, I know,' said the man; 'but he'll be quiet for a while now. We'll get the nurse and the medicine as fast as we can.' He signalled me to

I SAW THE DOCTOR COME OUT OF THE COTTAGE FOLLOWED BY A
DRAGGLE-TAILED WENCH.

come forward with the car, and I strove
not to be privy to what followed. But
I saw the girl's face, blotched and frozen
with grief, and I felt the hand without
a ring clutching at my knees when we
moved away.

The Doctor was a man of some
humour, for I remember he claimed
my car under the Oath of Æsculapius,
and used it and me without mercy.
First we convoyed Mrs. Madehurst and
the blind woman to wait by the sick
bed till the nurse should come. Next
we invaded a neat county town for pre-
scriptions (the Doctor said the trouble
was cerebro-spinal meningitis), and when
the County Institute, banked and flanked
with scared market cattle, reported itself
out of nurses for the moment we
literally flung ourselves loose upon the
county. We conferred with the owners
of great houses—magnates at the ends

of overarching avenues whose big-boned
womenfolk strode away from their tea-
tables to listen to the imperious Doctor.
At last a white-haired lady sitting under
a cedar of Lebanon and surrounded by
a court of magnificent Borzois—all
hostile to motors—gave the Doctor,
who received them as from a princess,
written orders which we bore many
miles at top speed, through a park, to a
French nunnery, where we took over
in exchange a pallid-faced and trembling
Sister. She knelt at the bottom of the
tonneau telling her beads without pause
till, by short-cuts of the Doctor's
invention, we had her to the sweetmeat
shop once more. It was a long afternoon
crowded with mad episodes that rose
and dissolved like the dust of our wheels ;
cross-sections of remote and incompre-
hensible lives through which we raced
at right angles ; and I went home in

F

AT LAST A WHITE-HAIRED LADY SITTING UNDER A CEDAR OF LEBANON.

the dusk, wearied out, to dream of the clashing horns of cattle ; round-eyed nuns walking in a garden of graves ; pleasant tea-parties beneath shaded trees ; the carbolic-scented, grey-painted corridors of the County Institute ; the steps of shy children in the wood, and the hands that clung to my knees as the motor began to move.

 . . . . .

I had intended to return in a day or two, but it pleased Fate to hold me from that side of the county, on many pretexts, till the elder and the wild rose had fruited. There came at last a brilliant day, swept clear from the south-west, that brought the hills within hand's reach—a day of unstable airs and high filmy clouds. Through no merit of my own I was free, and set the car for the third time on that known road. As I reached the crest of the Downs

I felt the soft air change, saw it glaze
under the sun ; and, looking down at
the sea, in that instant beheld the blue
of the Channel turn through polished
silver and dulled steel to dingy pewter.
A laden collier hugging the coast steered
outward for deeper water, and, across
copper-coloured haze, I saw sails rise
one by one on the anchored fishing-fleet.
In a deep dene behind me an eddy of
sudden wind drummed through sheltered
oaks, and spun aloft the first dry sample
of autumn leaves. When I reached
the beach road the sea-fog fumed over
the brickfields, and the tide was telling
all the groins of the gale beyond
Ushant. In less than an hour summer
England vanished in chill grey. We
were again the shut island of the
North, all the ships of the world
bellowing at our perilous gates ; and
between their outcries ran the piping

of bewildered gulls. My cap dripped
moisture, the folds of the rug held it in
pools or sluiced it away in runnels, and
the salt-rime stuck to my lips.

Inland the smell of autumn loaded
the thickened fog among the trees, and
the drip became a continuous shower.
Yet the late flowers—mallow of the
wayside, scabious of the field, and dahlia
of the garden—showed gay in the mist,
and beyond the sea's breath there was
little sign of decay in the leaf. Yet
in the villages the house doors were
all open, and bare-legged, bare-headed
children sat at ease on the damp door-
steps to shout 'pip-pip' at the stranger.

I made bold to call at the sweetmeat
shop, where Mrs. Madehurst met me
with a fat woman's hospitable tears.
Jenny's child, she said, had died two
days after the nun had come. It was,
she felt, best out of the way, even though

insurance offices, for reasons which she
did not pretend to follow, would not
willingly insure such stray lives. 'Not
but what Jenny didn't tend to Arthur
as though he'd come all proper at de
end of de first year—like Jenny herself.'
Thanks to Miss Florence, the child had
been buried with a pomp which, in
Mrs. Madehurst's opinion, more than
covered the small irregularity of its birth.
She described the coffin, within and
without, the glass hearse, and the ever-
green lining of the grave.

'But how's the mother?' I asked.

'Jenny?   Oh, she'll get over it.
I've felt dat way with one or two o' my
own. She'll get over. She's walkin'
in de wood now.'

'In this weather?'

Mrs. Madehurst looked at me with
narrowed eyes across the counter.

'I dunno but it opens de 'eart

"I DUNNO BUT IT OPENS DE 'EART LIKE. YES, IT OPENS DE 'EART."

like.   Yes, it opens de 'eart.   Dat's
where losin' and bearin' comes so alike
in de long run, we do say.'

Now the wisdom of the old wives is
greater than that of all the Fathers, and
this last oracle sent me thinking so ex-
tendedly as I went up the road, that I
nearly ran over a woman and a child at
the wooded corner by the lodge gates
of the House Beautiful.

'Awful weather !' I cried, as I
slowed dead for the turn.

'Not so bad,' she answered placidly
out of the fog.   'Mine's used to
'un.   You'll find yours indoors, I
reckon.'

Indoors, Madden received me with
professional courtesy, and kind inquiries
for the health of the motor, which he
would put under cover.

I waited in a still, nut-brown hall,
pleasant with late flowers and warmed

with a delicious wood fire—a place of
good influence and great peace. (Men
and women may sometimes, after great
effort, achieve a creditable lie ; but the
house, which is their temple, cannot
tell anything save the truth of those
who have lived in it.)   A child's cart
and a doll lay on the black-and-white˙
floor, where a rug had been kicked back.
I felt that the children had only just
hurried away—to hide themselves, most
like, in the many turns of the great
adzed staircase that climbed statelily
out of the hall, or to crouch at gaze
behind the lions and roses of the carven
gallery above.   Then I heard her voice
above me, singing as the blind sing—
from the soul :—

In the pleasant orchard-closes.

And all my early summer came back at
the call.

> In the pleasant orchard-closes,
> God bless all our gains say we—
> But may God bless all our losses,
> Better suits with our degree.

She dropped the marring fifth line, and repeated—

> Better suits with our degree !

I saw her lean over the gallery, her linked hands white as pearl against the oak.

'Is that you—from the other side of the county ? ' she called.

'Yes, me—from the other side of the county,' I answered, laughing.

'What a long time before you had to come here again.' She ran down the stairs, one hand lightly touching the broad rail. 'It's two months and four days. Summer's gone ! '

'I meant to come before, but Fate prevented.'

'I knew it. Please do something to that fire. They won't let me play with it, but I can feel it's behaving badly. Hit it!'

I looked on either side of the deep fireplace, and found but a half-charred hedge-stake with which I punched a black log into flame.

'It never goes out, day or night,' she said, as though explaining. 'In case any one comes in with cold toes, you see.'

'It's even lovelier inside than it was out,' I murmured. The red light poured itself along the age-polished dusky panels till the Tudor roses and lions of the gallery took colour and motion. An old eagle-topped convex mirror gathered the picture into its mysterious heart, distorting afresh the distorted shadows, and curving the gallery lines into the curves of a ship.

The day was shutting down in half a gale as the fog turned to stringy scud. Through the uncurtained mullions of the broad window I could see the valiant horsemen of the lawn rear and recover against the wind that pelted them with legions of dead leaves.

'Yes, it must be beautiful,' she said. 'Would you like to go over it? There's still light enough upstairs.'

I followed her up the unflinching, wagon-wide staircase to the gallery whence opened the thin fluted Elizabethan doors.

'Feel how they put the latches low down for the sake of the children.' She swung a light door inward.

'By the way, where are they?' I asked. 'I haven't even heard them to-day.'

She did not answer at once. Then, 'I can only hear them,' she replied

softly. 'This is one of their rooms—
everything ready, you see.'

She pointed into a heavily-timbered
room. There were little low gate-
tables and children's chairs. A doll's
house, its hooked front half open, faced
a great dappled rocking-horse, from
whose padded saddle it was but a child's
scramble to the broad window-seat
overlooking the lawn. A toy gun
lay in a corner beside a gilt wooden
cannon.

'Surely they've only just gone,' I
whispered. In the failing light a door
creaked cautiously. I heard the rustle
of a frock and the patter of feet—quick
feet through a room beyond.

'I heard that!' she cried triumphantly.
'Did you? Children, oh, children!
Where are you?'

The voice filled the walls that held
it lovingly to the last perfect note, but

"THIS IS ONE OF THEIR ROOMS—EVERYTHING READY, YOU SEE."

there came no answering shout such as
I had heard in the garden.   We hurried
on from room to oak-floored room ; up
a step here, down three steps there ;
among a maze of passages ; always
mocked by our quarry.   One might as
well have tried to work an unstopped
warren with a single ferret.   There
were bolt-holes innumerable—recesses
in walls, embrasures of deep-slitten
windows now filled up, whence they
could start up behind us; and abandoned
fireplaces, six feet deep in the masonry,
as well as the tangle of communicating
doors.   Above all, they had the twilight
for their helper in our game.   I had
caught one or two joyous chuckles of
evasion, and once or twice had seen the
silhouette of a child's frock against some
darkening window at the end of a
passage ; but we returned empty-handed
to the gallery, just as a middle-aged

woman was setting a lamp in its niche.

'No, I haven't seen her either this evening, Miss Florence,' I heard her say, 'but that Turpin he says he wants to see you about his shed.'

'Oh, Mr. Turpin must want to see me very badly. Tell him to come to the hall, Mrs. Madden.'

I looked down into the hall whose only light was the dulled fire; and deep in the shadow I saw them at last. They must have slipped down while we were in the passages, and now thought themselves perfectly hidden behind an old gilt leather screen. By child's law, my fruitless chase was as good as an introduction, but since I had taken so much trouble, I resolved to force them to come forward later by the trick, which children detest, of pretending not to notice them. They lay close, in a

THEY MUST HAVE SLIPPED DOWN WHILE WE WERE IN THE PASSAGES.

little huddle, no more than shadows
except when a quick flame betrayed a
small outline.

'And now we'll have some tea,' she
said. 'I believe I ought to have offered
it you at first, but one doesn't arrive at
manners somehow when one lives alone
and is considered — h'm — peculiar.'
Then with a very pretty scorn, 'Would
you like a lamp to see to eat by ?'

'The firelight's much pleasanter, I
think.' We descended into that delicious gloom and Madden brought tea.

I took my chair in the direction of
the screen ready to surprise or be surprised as the game should go, and at
her permission, since the hearth is always
sacred, bent forward to play with the fire.

'Where do you get these beautiful
short faggots from ?' I asked idly.
'Why, they are tallies !'

'Of course,' she replied. 'As I can't

"WOULD YOU LIKE A LAMP TO SEE TO EAT BY?"

read or write I'm driven back on the early English tally for my accounts. Give me one and I'll tell you what it meant.'

I passed her an unburned hazel-tally, about a foot long, and she ran her thumb down the nicks.

'This is the milk-record for the home farm for the month of April last year, in gallons,' said she. 'I don't know what I should have done without tallies. An old forester of mine taught me the system. It's out of date now for every one else; but my tenants respect it. One of them's coming now to see me. Oh, it doesn't matter. He has no business here out of office hours. He's a greedy, ignorant man — very greedy or—he wouldn't come here after dark.'

'Have you much land then?'

'Only a couple of hundred acres in

hand, thank goodness. The other six hundred are nearly all let to folk who knew my folk before me ; but this Turpin is quite a new man—and a highway robber.'

'But are you sure I shan't be—— ? '

'Certainly not. You have the right. He hasn't any children.'

'Ah, the children !' I said, and slid my low chair back till it nearly touched the screen that hid them. 'I wonder whether they'll come out for me.'

There was a murmur of voices— Madden's and a deeper note—at the low, dark side door, and a ginger-headed, canvas-gaitered giant of the unmistakable tenant-farmer type stumbled or was pushed in.

'Come to the fire, Mr. Turpin,' she said.

'If—if you please, Miss, I'll—I'll be quite as well by the door.' He clung

to the latch as he spoke like a frightened
child. Of a sudden I realised that he
was in the grip of some almost over-
powering fear.

' Well ? '

' About that new shed for the young
stock—that was all. These first autumn
storms settin' in . . . but I'll come
again, Miss.' His teeth did not chatter
much more than the door-latch.

' I think not,' she answered levelly.
' The new shed—m'm. What did my
agent write you on the 15th ? '

' I—fancied p'raps that if I came to
see you—ma—man to man like, Miss.
But——'

His eyes rolled into every corner of
the room wide with horror. He half
opened the door through which he had
entered, but I noticed that it was shut
again—from without and firmly.

' He wrote what I told him,' she

H

went on. 'You are overstocked already. Dunnett's Farm never carried more than fifty bullocks—even in Mr. Wright's time. And *he* used cake. You've sixty-seven and you don't cake. You've broken the lease in that respect. You're dragging the heart out of the farm.'

'I'm—I'm getting some minerals—superphosphates—next week. I've as good as ordered a truck-load already. I'll go down to the station to-morrow about 'em. Then I can come and see you man to man like, Miss, in the daylight. . . . That gentleman's not going away, is he?' He almost shrieked.

I had only slid the chair a little farther back, reaching behind me to tap on the leather of the screen, but he jumped like a rat.

'No. Please attend to me, Mr.

Turpin.' She turned in her chair and
faced him with his back to the door.
It was an old and sordid little piece of
scheming that she forced from him—
his plea for the new cow-shed at his land-
lady's expense, that he might with the
covered manure pay his next year's rent
out of the valuation after, as she made
clear, he had bled the enriched pastures
to the bone. I could not but admire
the intensity of his greed, when I saw
him out-facing for its sake whatever
terror it was that ran wet on his forehead.

I ceased to tap the leather—was, indeed, calculating the cost of the shed—
when I felt my relaxed hand taken and
turned softly between the soft hands of
a child. So at last I had triumphed.
In a moment I would turn and ac-
quaint myself with those quick-footed
wanderers. . . .

The little brushing kiss fell in the centre of my palm—as a gift on which the fingers were, once, expected to close: as the all-faithful half-reproachful signal of a waiting child not used to neglect even when grown-ups were busiest—a fragment of the mute code devised very long ago.

Then I knew. Then it was as though I had known from the first day when I looked across the lawn at the high window.

I heard the door shut. The woman turned to me in silence, and I felt that she knew.

What time passed after this I cannot say. I was roused by the fall of a log, and mechanically rose to put it back. Then I returned to my place in the chair very close to the screen.

'Now you understand,' she whispered, across the packed shadows.

THE LITTLE BRUSHING KISS FELL IN THE CENTRE OF MY PALM.

'Yes, I understand—now. Thank you.'

'I—I only hear them.' She bowed her head in her hands. 'I have no right, you know—no other right. I have neither borne nor lost—neither borne nor lost!'

'Be very glad then,' said I, for my soul was torn open within me.

'Forgive me!'

She was still, and I went back to my sorrow and my joy.

'It was because I loved them so,' she said at last, brokenly. '*That* was why it was, even from the first—even before I knew that they—they were all I should ever have. And I loved them so!'

She stretched out her arms to the shadows and the shadows within the shadow.

'They came because I loved them— because I needed them. I—I must

have made them come. Was that wrong, think you? Did I wrong any one?'

' No—no!'

' I—I grant you that the toys and—and all that sort of thing were nonsense, but—but I used to so hate empty rooms myself when I was little.' She pointed to the gallery. 'And the passages all empty. . . . And how could I ever bear the garden door shut? Suppose——'

' Don't! For pity's sake, don't!' I cried. The twilight had brought a cold rain with gusty squalls that plucked at the leaded windows.

' And the same thing with keeping the fire in all night. *I* don't think it so foolish—do you?'

I looked at the broad brick hearth; saw, through tears I believe, that there was no unpassable iron on or near it; and bowed my head.

' I did all that and lots of other things
—just to make believe. Then they
came. I heard them, but I didn't know
that they were not mine by right till
Mrs. Madden told me——'

'The butler's wife? What?'

'One of them—I heard—she saw.
And knew. Hers! *Not* for me. I
didn't know at first. Perhaps I was
jealous. Afterwards, I began to understand that it was only because I loved
them, not because—— . . . Oh, you
must bear or lose,' she said piteously.
'There is no other way. And yet they
love me. They must! Don't they?'

There was no sound in the room
except the lapping voices of the fire, but
we two listened intently, and she, at least,
took comfort from what she heard. She
recovered herself and half rose. I sat
still in my chair by the screen.

'Don't think me a wretch to whine

"AND YET THEY LOVE ME, THEY MUST! DON'T THEY?"

about myself like this, but—but I'm all in the dark, you know, and *you* can see.'

In truth I could see, and my vision confirmed me in my resolve, though that was like the very parting of spirit and flesh. Yet a little longer I would stay since it was the last time.

'You think it is wrong, then?' she cried sharply, though I had said nothing.

'Not for you. A thousand times no. For you it is right. . . . I am grateful to you beyond words. For me it would be wrong. For me only. . . .'

'Why?' she said, but passed her hand before her face as she had done at our second meeting in the wood. 'Oh, I see,' she went on simply as a child. 'For you it would be wrong.' Then with a little indrawn laugh, 'and, d'you remember, I called you lucky—once—

at first. You who must never come here again!"

She left me to sit a little longer by the screen, and I heard her feet die out along the gallery above.

CPSIA information can be obtained
at www.ICGtesting.com
Printed in the USA
LVHW081516240622
722064LV00002B/18